Ruby Rogers
Get Me Out of Here!

Sue Limb

Illustrations by Bernice Lum

BLOOMSBURY

First published in Great Britain in 2008 by Bloomsbury Publishing Plc
36 Soho Square, London, WID 3QY

A CIP catalogue record of this book is available from the British Library

ISBN 978 0 7475 9248 8

All papers used by Bloomsbury Publishing are natural, recyclable
products made from wood grown in well-managed forests.
The manufacturing processes conform to the environmental
regulations of the country of origin.

Printed in Great Britain by Clays Ltd, St Ives Plc

1 3 5 7 9 10 8 6 4 2

www.suelimb.com
www.bloomsbury.com

I couldn't believe it!

'THERE'S A fallen tree!' Mum and I ran down to the front gate to have a look at the damage. The tree was lying right across our driveway. Some of its roots were torn and twisted and sticking in the air. It looked wrong on the ground – like somebody who's fallen over. I felt as if I was going to cry.

'It looks like a hurricane's been down the street!' said Mum. 'Oh dear! I hate it when trees are uprooted like that!'

All night the wind had been roaring and crashing around the house. I could hear things blowing about in the garden. There was thunder and lightning too. It was terrifying. I'd hid my head under the covers and held on tight to my monkeys.

'We won't be able to get the car out,' said Mum. 'I'll have to ring Alison and ask if she can give me a lift to work – and you'll have to walk to school, Ruby.'

We went back indoors to get everything sorted. I had managed not to cry, but I felt kind of sick and wrong. I could always save it up to cry about later. If you don't let a cry out, it can poison you – worse than Dad's lasagne (but that's another story).

It's not very far to school. I nearly always walk home from school anyway. But I usually get a lift in the mornings because we're always in a rush, and, somehow, my sports kit is always in the fruit bowl and my library book's down the loo or something.

'Where's my mobile? Where's my mobile? Where's my mobile?' That was Dad panicking in the kitchen. I take after Dad. We're both untidy. Mum's not always completely on our side.

'How should I know?' she snapped. 'Where's your bag, Ruby? Get a move on, or you'll be late!'

'It's a good excuse, though,' I said, picking up my bag. 'Mrs Jenkins won't be cross if I tell her we were trapped by a tree.'

'Never mind that!' said Mum. 'Get a move on!'

'Ah!' cried Dad. 'Found it! In my pocket. How bizarre.'

I kissed Mum and Dad goodbye and went off down the path. 'Don't accept any lifts from strangers!' called Mum. She gets panic attacks sometimes, after something awful has been on the TV news.

I was really looking forward to the walk to school. Squeezing past the fallen tree was an interesting challenge. I felt as if I was on some kind of wildlife documentary. And it was exciting, in an awful kind of way, to see lots of roof tiles lying in the street, and bits of wood and plastic blowing about.

Joe was still in bed, missing all the drama. Now he's finished his A levels he doesn't have to go to school any more. So he's on 'study leave' – another term for sleeping.

As I turned into the main road I saw my role model, Holly Helvellyn, strolling along. She doesn't lie in bed till midday. She goes to school anyway, even though she's finished her A levels too. I think she likes to use the art room at Ashcroft School, because they've got all the latest arty materials there.

'Hi, Ruby!' she called. 'Amazing storm, wasn't it? I couldn't believe it! The house next to ours was struck by lighting and the chimney pot fell off. Thank goodness nobody was standing in their garden at the time!'

'I heard on the news,' I said, 'that somebody was killed by a falling tree in Birmingham. It's horrible, these storms.'

'Climate change,' said Holly grimly. 'Global warming. We've got to get to grips with it.'

I hoped she wouldn't talk about climate change too much, because I was more interested in something else.

'Joe's still asleep!' I said. 'He missed all the action! He doesn't get up till lunchtime these days.'

'Lazy bones,' smiled Holly.

I waited, but she didn't say anything else. Joe and Holly seemed to get on really well at my party recently. We all sat in the garden and wore masks and Holly lit candles. She organises great parties.

But I still wasn't sure if she and Joe were just ordinary friends, or something else.

'Does Dom lie in bed till lunchtime too?' I asked cunningly. 'Is it a boy thing?'

Holly shrugged. She certainly didn't light up at the mention of Dom's name. (He's her ex, at least, I hope he's still her ex – that's what I was trying to find out.) She frowned, as if a little black cloud crossed over her face at the thought of him.

'I haven't seen him for a while,' she said sourly, 'and that suits me fine. That guy was such a poser! I don't even go anywhere near Beaubridge any more.'

'Is that where he lives?' I asked.

'Yes,' said Holly. Then she kind of went off into a thoughtful mood. She seemed to have forgotten about me. I was beginning to regret having mentioned Dom. Maybe she was remembering all the good times they'd had. Maybe she was missing him. Maybe they would get back together again, and it would all be my fault!

'Tiffany never comes anywhere near our house now, either,' I said, reminding her tactfully that Joe and Tiffany had split up too. So now was her chance to grab my smelly, lazy brother. She didn't look very excited at the idea. Who would?

'So, what's cooking this week, then, Ruby?' Holly had kind of shaken herself out of her quiet mood.

'It's Yasmin's birthday party on Saturday,' I told her.

'Oh yes! What are you giving her?' asked Holly.

My heart sank. I'd been trying not to think about this.

'I don't know,' I sighed. 'Hannah's giving her some really amazing clothes, or something, and Lauren's going to offer her some riding lessons on her pony. I can't compete with that! Plus I forgot to save up my pocket money and I'm totally broke.'

'Why don't you make her something?' said Holly thoughtfully. 'Handmade things are so classy and really touching.'

'But what could I make?' I was beginning to feel quite anxious and stressy about Yasmin's birthday. 'I'm useless at making things.'

'Don't be silly, Ruby,' said Holly. 'You're brilliant. You really like painting. What's the problem?'

'Please will you help me, then?' I asked. 'Maybe you could come over one night after school this week?'

Holly pulled a slightly mysterious face and

shook her head doubtfully. I just knew it was something to do with Joe.

'I'm a bit busy this week, Ruby,' she said. 'I've promised my mum I'll help her in her gallery after school. She's got a new exhibition to set up for Friday and her assistant's got flu.'

'Oh no!' I wailed. 'I can't do it on my own! I've got, like, no ideas. My mind is totally blank.'

'Don't be silly, Rube,' she smiled. 'You'll think of something.'

CHAPTER 2
Yesssssss!

AT MID-MORNING break, Yasmin and I were in our favourite corner of the school-yard, under a little tree. I like shady places. And I love trees.

'I'm so pleased you weren't blown over!' I told the tree. I threw my arms around the trunk and gave it a hug. 'Trees are my friends!'

'What about your *proper* friends?' snapped Yasmin. She sounded a little bit stressy. She was unwrapping her mum's divine cheese sandwiches, so I had to be careful not to irritate her.

'There's no need to be jealous of a tree!' I grinned, letting go of the trunk. 'I'll give you two hugs for every hug I give this tree. How about that?'

'Ugh, no, back off, Ruby – you've got dirt and green stuff all over you!'

I looked down. The moss and lichen from the tree trunk was still wet from last night's storm. And now it was all down my front.

'I don't care!' I said. 'I do love trees, though. I hate it when they get blown over. Are all the trees in your garden all right?'

'Shut up about trees,' snapped Yasmin. She'd got the sandwiches out now. They lay there on the foil like two divine little soft white beds. She offered them to me. I picked the nearest one. (Mum has trained me to do that.)

'Thanks so much!' I drooled. 'Oh, your mum's sandwiches are absolute heaven! Is she making them for the party? I can hardly wait!'

Yasmin looked pleased because I'd praised her mum's sandwiches. Mrs Saffet really is a brilliant cook. She sometimes makes traditional Turkish cakes and I was looking forward to Yasmin's party as a chance to eat till I popped.

'There's going to be masses and masses of

yummy scrumptious things!' said Yasmin. Her eyes
started to sparkle. 'There's going to be special little
individual cheese tarts and cheese straws and stuff.
And my granny's coming over from Turkey and
she'll be bringing some dolmades.'

I tried not to look scared at the thought of
Yasmin's granny. She's quite a big old lady and
whenever she sees me she throws her arms around
me and crushes me into a small heap. It's like being
loved by a concrete mixer. Also, she likes pinching
children. Why do that? Why not just give them a
smile or, even better, a pocket-sized monkey?

'And the cakes!' Yasmin went on, rolling her
eyes in delight. 'Honey cakes, chocolate cakes,
iced cakes and those lovely apple and cinnamon

pastries – oh my God! I feel faint just thinking about it!'

'So do I,' I said. 'Your party's going to be the best ever!'

'Yessss!' hissed Yasmin. 'Oh, but your party was lovely too, Ruby!'

'It was OK.' I shrugged. 'But only because Holly came and rescued it with the masks and the candles and stuff. I don't mind. I don't really like giving parties. I prefer going to other people's. Yours is going to be brilliant!'

Yasmin jumped up and down, which was a mistake so soon after her cheese sandwich. She got the hiccups.

'What are you going to give me as a present – hic!?' she demanded.

I panicked slightly. I'm not much good at giving people presents *or* throwing a party. Since talking to Holly, I still hadn't come up with any ideas at all for Yasmin's present.

'It's a secret,' I said.

'Oh – hic!' Yasmin looked thrilled. 'A secret! Is it big or small? Would it fit in a jewel box or a shoe box? Or a cardboard carton like Mum uses for bringing the groceries home – hic!?' I tried to look secretive and mysterious. 'Not that it has to be big!'

Yasmin went on. 'I didn't mean that, honestly, Ruby. It's fine if it's small! In fact, sometimes the best presents are – hic! – tiny!'

'Let's go and get you a drink of water,' I said, trying to change the subject. 'Apparently, if you drink a glass of water backwards, it'll cure hiccups.' We walked into the girls' cloakrooms. 'Or if that doesn't work, we can go to the staffroom and ask for a paper bag,' I went on. 'If you breathe in and out of a paper bag, it can cure hiccups. My dad made me do it last time.'

'Hannah's getting me something to do with clothes,' said Yasmin excitedly. She wasn't even listening to my speech about hiccup cures. Well, I wasn't even listening to it myself. It was dead boring. I was really racking my brains about what my amazing secret present could possibly be. 'And Lauren's is something to do with – hic! – ponies. She's not *actually* going to give me an *actual* pony, of course – imagine trying to wrap it up!'

Then she started to giggle, and it got more and more hysterical what with the hiccups as well, and when she tried to drink a bit of water she choked, and some of it came down her nose.

'Help – hic!' screamed Yasmin, holding on to the

rim of the washbasin. 'I nearly drowned then! Hic! Oh heck! I'm going to be – hic – in a minute!'

'I was hic last Christmas,' I said. 'Too many chocolates.'

Yasmin went off into another huge fit of the giggles. I wondered if I could give her a box of chocolates. I could borrow the money from Mum or maybe Joe. Chocolates didn't seem like a very good present, though, because once you've eaten them there's no present left.

'Think of something sad,' I suggested. I could see Yas was pretty hysterical now, and I didn't want her to actually be sick, or even hic. It's not my favourite spectator sport. I'd even rather watch cricket. 'Think of starving children in Africa.' Yasmin's giggles began to slow down. 'With big, dark, tragic eyes,' I added. Yasmin stopped laughing completely.

'Thanks, Ruby,' she said. Then she sighed and washed her face. You know how it is after the giggles – you feel kind of heavy and twisted and empty. We walked back outside. Yasmin put her arm round me.

'Do you think it's very bad to have parties when there are starving children in Africa?' she said, staring gloomily at the ground.

'No,' I said firmly. 'After we've had the party, next week we can raise some money for the starving children in Africa.' Yasmin cheered up a bit at this idea.

'Yeah, that's right,' she said. 'Thanks, Ruby – you've been great.' I felt quite grown-up and kind of grand and clever for a split second. 'Just tell me one thing,' Yasmin went on. 'This present you've got me – which size box could it fit into? Could it fix into a shoe box? Yes or no?'

'You wouldn't put it in a box at all,' I said recklessly, desperately saying the first thing that came into my head. Yasmin's eyes flared wide.

'*You wouldn't put it in a box?*' she repeated, like somebody hypnotised. 'Oh, how *amazing*! I wonder what it can possibly be.'

She gazed into my eyes as if she was trying to read my mind. Just as well she couldn't. I was in worse trouble than ever. Before, I'd just not got her a present yet, while pretending that I had. Now, I had to get her the kind of present that you wouldn't put in a box. Why did I have to open my big mouth?

CHAPTER 3

But what can I get her?

THAT EVENING, after I'd finished my homework, I made a list of everything Yasmin likes in the hope that it might inspire a present idea. It went like this:

Clothes
Fashion
Animals
Chocolate
Jewellery
TV comedy, especially The Simpsons
Shrek

Magic
Ghosts

Yasmin certainly has plenty of interests. I looked at the list. I'd have liked to get her a DVD of *The Simpsons*, but I only had £2.50 saved up. Besides, you could put a DVD into a box. I had to get her something you couldn't fit in a box.

I went downstairs with my list. Everybody was sitting out in the back garden, having a drink and admiring Dad's roses.

'Where have you been, Ruby?' said Mum sleepily, reaching out an arm to me. She was in the old-fashioned deckchair. I gave her a hug – well, about

half a hug, which is all you can give somebody in a deckchair without causing an accident.

'Doing my homework,' I said in a goody-goody sort of voice.

'Oh, good girl, well done, petal,' said Mum.

'Please will you give me some money to buy Yasmin a present?' I asked. 'Her birthday's this Saturday and I've only got £2.50.'

Mum looked a tiny bit annoyed.

'I've told you before, Ruby, you should save up your pocket money – not all of it, just a pound a week would do. If you'd saved up a pound a week since Christmas, you'd have over £25 by now.'

'Sorry,' I said. 'I promise I will save it up from now on. What can I give her, though?'

'Try the charity shop,' said Dad. 'There's loads of stuff in there for less than £2.50. Mum bought me this shirt for £1.'

I looked at Dad's shirt. It was sky blue with elephants on it. OK for gardening, I suppose.

'It's got to be the sort of present you couldn't put in a box, though,' I told them.

'Why?' asked Mum.

'Because she kept asking me what my present was, and what size box it would fit into. In the end I got kind of fed up with it and I said it was the sort of thing you wouldn't put in a box at all.'

'You could give her a hyena,' said Joe. 'It would be quite a struggle trying to put a hyena in a box.'

'Or a snake,' said Dad.

'No,' said Joe. 'People put snakes in boxes all the time.'

'I wish all snakes were in boxes,' said Mum with a shudder.

'But what can I get her?' I wailed. This conversation wasn't helping me at all. 'I've made a list of things she likes, but just the card will cost most of what I've got saved up.'

'It's your own fault for not looking after your money properly,' said Mum. Sometimes she gets into these really strict moods.

'Let's see your list, then,' said Joe. I handed him the piece of paper and he skimmed through it. 'Get her a ghost,' he said, handing it back. 'You could never get a ghost into a box.'

I sighed. I was feeling quite stressy about the whole thing. Nobody was being any help at all.

'There's no need to waste your money on a card,' said Dad. 'Make her one.'

'Yes!' agreed Mum. 'Home-made cards are so much nicer. And you're quite good at painting, Ruby.'

'Have we got any white card?' I asked.

Joe came in with me and found lots of card and some paints. He gave me some rough paper too. He's quite arty — in fact, he's going to art college in the autumn and you can't get more arty than that. I spread newspaper over the dining-room table, laid out all my materials, and sat down and had a think.

I tried to draw Yasmin's face on the rough paper. It was really hard. The eyes were right, but the nose was more like a koala bear's. I tried again. This time the nose was fine, but the mouth was something like a post box. The third time I got the

mouth right, but the eyes were like those of a mad leopard out of a comic.

I went upstairs to my room and got out my box of photographs. There was a photo there of Yasmin and me on our school trip. I had my eyes closed and my mouth open, but Yasmin looked really pretty.

I took it downstairs and photocopied it on our great all-in-one printer. Then I cut Yasmin's face out of the photocopy version and stuck it in the middle of a big white sheet of card. It was a really, really *huge* sheet of card, bigger than the biggest pizza you could imagine, and, of course, square.

Now Yasmin's face was grinning at me out of a vast white space. It was odd, but interesting. On a piece of rough paper, I tried to draw a fabulous dress, the sort a film star would wear to the Oscars. But it was rubbish. It looked like a pair of curtains. I was never going to be world famous fashion designer.

In the kitchen we have a cardboard box where the old papers and magazines are kept so we can recycle them. I had a look through them and straight away I found lots of photos of celebrities going to some premiere or other.

I took the whole page back to the table and

compared the celebs' dresses with the face of Yasmin till I found one that was just about the right size. It was Scarlett Johansson in a fabulous green slinky satin number. I'm not great on clothes but even I could see it was stunning. Carefully, I cut out the whole of Scarlett from the neck down, leaving her head behind, and arranged the body of the cinema goddess on the white card below the head of my best buddy.

It was amazing! It fitted exactly! It looked as if Yasmin was a film star! I was thrilled. This was going to be the best card ever. If my card was totally cool, maybe Yasmin wouldn't mind if my present was a bit boring.

At this point Mum came in and made a lot of fuss about how late it was and how these light evenings were awful because you sat about in the garden and suddenly it was half past nine, and I must go to bed now, etc. etc. etc.

She did admire my card, though. I put it away safely so I could work on it again tomorrow night.

It was quite hard to get to sleep, as ideas kept buzzing around in my head. Because the card was so enormous, there was room for all Yasmin's favourite things on it. It could have clothes and fashion and chocolate and animals on it. *And* jewellery *and* TV comedy *and* Shrek. *And* ghosts *and* magic! If I couldn't find pictures of these things in magazines, then I would just draw them myself. I really hoped Yasmin would like it. Because if she didn't – well, I couldn't bear to think about that.

CHAPTER 4
How amazing!

EVERY EVENING for the next few days, as soon as I'd finished my homework, I went to work on Yasmin's card. Except it wasn't just a card now. It was more like the sort of picture you put on the wall.

'It's an Old Master,' said Dad, admiring it on Thursday after the TV news. 'Or I suppose you could call it a Young Miss.'

'You should sell it at Sotheby's,' said Joe. 'It would probably fetch thousands.'

I didn't mind being teased, because I was so

pleased with it. In the middle was Yasmin wearing her Oscar dress. All around her were things she loved. There were bluebirds, pink stars, cheese sandwiches, zany dolls and polka-dot rabbits wearing pearl earrings. There was a ghost in high-heels wearing shiny pale blue clouds and fabulous bling. Shrek was there, peeping out of an egg. (Yasmin loves boiled eggs.) There was a glamorous witch with a sparkly wand and stars and moons and rockets. Tucked away in a corner was a funny animal made up of my head and a monkey's body. So I was there too.

I'd cut up loads and loads of magazines, drawn things with my sparkly pens, and even stuck on sequins and bits of lace. I was so thrilled with it, I just couldn't stop looking at it.

'I'll get you a big envelope,' said Mum. 'It's beautiful, Ruby! Well done!' I had one niggling little worry, though.

'But it's still just a card,' I said. 'I should give her a proper present too, or it won't be fair.' Mum looked thoughtful.

'Well, as you've worked so hard,' she said, 'I'll give you some money to buy Yasmin a little present – nothing fancy, mind! We'll go into town on Saturday morning.'

This was a bit last minute, but we are a bit of a last-minute family. On Saturday Mum and I went out to the shops.

'It has to be something you can't put in a box,' I reminded her, 'because I said that to Yasmin when she kept on and on asking me what it was.'

Mum laughed.

'Don't be silly, Ruby,' she said. 'Look at these lovely books!'

We were in a shop that sold lots of different sorts of things to do with paper – files and books to write in, and sparkly paper decorations and stuff. Just the sort of thing Yasmin likes.

Mum showed me a beautiful notebook. The cover was decorated with an angel's face, all done in gold and silver with glittering wings in the background. It had a clasp and a key so you could write the most secret things and then lock the book and nobody would be able to read it. It was perfect for Yasmin. She's obsessed with secrets.

We bought the book and some wrapping paper with hippos wearing tutus and doing ballet, and some fancy ribbon. Once we'd got it home and wrapped it up, it looked amazing. But I was still busy with the card, putting finishing touches to it. I wrote *HAPPY BIRTHDAY, YASMIN* in gold letters on it. I couldn't wait to see her face when she saw it. But I was glad we'd got a proper present too.

'OK,' said Mum at half past three. 'You'd better get changed into some party clothes, Ruby.'

I do have a party dress but I don't really like wearing it because it's just not my style. My granny bought it for me so I have to wear it when she comes, which isn't very often, thank goodness. Today I selected my best green shorts and a stripy zebra T-shirt.

Dad drove me to Yasmin's. As I got out of the car I could hear music and a lot of happy shouting and laughing inside the house. The front door was open and there was a bunch of balloons tied to the gate. My heart started to beat very fast.

'OK, sweetheart!' said Dad with a grin. 'Go easy on the gin and tonic! I'll collect you at seven.' (That was a joke about the gin and tonic, of course. Even Dad never drinks gin and tonic.)

I walked up the path carrying the huge envelope and present. I didn't know whether to ring the bell or go straight in. I had a sudden stupid feeling of shyness and wanting to run away home. I heard my dad's car drive off. I was on my own.

Luckily Mrs Saffet appeared at the far end of

the hall and saw me standing on the doorstep like a nerd.

'Come in, Ruby!' she smiled, beckoning. 'They're all in the sitting room.'

I went in. Yasmin was sitting on the sofa, opening presents, surrounded by people. Her granny was sitting next to her. Practically our whole class was gathered round. When Yasmin throws a party, there's no holding back. The music was loud, and there was wrapping paper everywhere.

Yasmin didn't even hear me come in or see me, because there was so much noise and she was busy unwrapping a Gothic doll. Froggo was singing a song and dancing about. Max was imitating a jumbo jet taking off (he always does that when he feels a bit nervous). But Yasmin's granny looked up and saw me.

'Ruuuubih!' she yelled, and held out her arms. I had *so* got to go over and give her a kiss. How embarrassing.

I got dragged down on to the sofa into a kind of human tossed salad with Yasmin and her granny and Yasmin's sister, Zerrin. They all kissed me. The granny's kisses were like guided missiles. I struggled up for air. Yasmin had already grabbed the card and present.

'How amazing, Ruby!' she yelled, ripping open
the envelope and pulling the card out. She pulled
it out so fiercely that for a moment I was afraid
she was going to rip it. 'Wow! Look, Granny! Isn't
this card amazing? Ruby made it herself!'

Yasmin hugged me madly. The granny said,
'Bery cleber', which is a kind of Turkish way of
saying 'very clever'. Sometimes I wish one of my
grannies was foreign. It's so stylish.

Then Yasmin put the card to one side and
ripped open the present. The ribbons we'd spent
five minutes on were hurled to the carpet in sec-
onds. They were history.

'Wow, what an amazing book! It's *sooooooo* beautiful!' shouted Yasmin. She started fiddling with the lock. 'I can't wait to write in it!' she said excitedly. 'I'll write my first thing in it tonight! It'll be my secret diary!'

She'd spent a lot more time talking about the present than the card. What a good job I'd nagged Mum into getting her a proper present.

At this point Hannah arrived with a small envelope and a very big present. I saw Yasmin's granny pick up my card and add it to the pile of cards on her lap. But she put it at the bottom of the pile. I suppose it was because it was the biggest. I felt sad that she didn't want to look at it again. It was kind of forgotten already.

Yasmin unwrapped Hannah's present, shrieking in excitement. Everyone gathered round. It was the biggest present so far. Maybe that's why she was shrieking. Why hadn't she shrieked at my card? It was way bigger than anyone else's.

Inside the wrapping paper was a silver box, and when Yasmin took off the lid, there was pale pink tissue paper inside. Yasmin whipped off the tissue paper and lifted out a pink T-shirt with a pink lion on it.

'It's because your star sign is Leo!' said Hannah.

'You can make the eyes flash. There's a battery – you just switch it on – here.' She showed Yasmin how to make the lion's eyes flash. They flashed red on and off and on and off all the time. I have to admit it was amazing. Or possibly even amaaaaaaaaaazing.

Yasmin jumped off the sofa. 'I'm going to put it on now!' she yelled, and ran upstairs. I noticed that as she'd got up, she'd crushed the corner of my card.

'I'll take those, Mum,' said Yasmin's mum to the granny. She took the cards over to the mantelpiece and started to arrange them. When she got to my card, it toppled over. It was too big to stand up properly. Mrs Saffet put it down on the coffee table. She didn't even look at it properly.

I tried not to feel bad about all this, but it was hard.

CHAPTER 5
Great idea!

AFTER A WHILE I forgot about my
card, though. There was so much to do –
and so much to eat. Yasmin's mum organised hilarious games. My favourite was where we had to
invent TV adverts for really horrible things, such
as wasps' nests and maggot pie and concrete shoes.

The best thing, though, was something really
small and not expensive. It was the present from
Max. It was a set of false teeth made of plastic,
about the size of a real set, I suppose, but this one
had legs. You could wind it up and it walked

about. It was hysterical. I literally laughed till I cried. Yasmin had had loads of really big presents in huge boxes. She had a magic kit with loads of tricks, a dragon glove puppet, a collection of practical jokes, including sweets that turn your tongue blue, but the thing I liked best was the false teeth.

At the end of the party we all got a party bag with some cake and stretchy aliens and bubble pots. It had been a fantastic party, but it had to end sometime. Our parents arrived to pick us up.

When Yasmin kissed me goodbye, she whispered, 'Thanks so much for that fabulous card, Ruby – I'm going to frame it and hang it on my bedroom wall.'

I was pleased that she rated it. I would have been slightly sorry if I hadn't been able to see it again. It was strange – while I'd been making it I'd sort of got fond of it, as if it was a pet or something. I looked around as I left the sitting room, but I couldn't see my card anywhere. Never mind. Soon it would be on Yasmin's bedroom wall and I could see it again next time.

It was Mum who collected me, and though she was glad I'd enjoyed the party, she was anxious about getting to the supermarket before it closed, so when I told her about the hilarious false teeth she hardly seemed to be listening.

Sunday was a bit dull after Yasmin's sensational party, and it was raining, which made it worse. I had to do chores, such as tidying my room. Life seemed a bit flat. I moped about downstairs, playing video games and lying on the sofa. Then I went into the kitchen to see if there were any snacks available.

'What's wrong with Ruby?' asked Dad, coming in from his greenhouse with a mad happy gardening look in his eye.

'I'm bored,' I said.

'Hmmm,' said Dad, washing his hands. 'Seems to me you're experiencing your first hangover. What you need is an interest in growing vegetables.'

I did a small, soft little scream of disgust at the very idea.

'I don't think it's that,' said Mum, wiping down the work surfaces with a smile of satisfaction (what terrible boring things grown-ups enjoy, by the way). 'I think Ruby's fed up because she's finished her card and she hasn't got another project.'

'Great idea!' said Dad. 'You should start to make another card, Rube. Make one for me.'

I didn't really feel like it, but I got out my painting materials. There was a bit of card left and plenty of rough paper. I tried to think of an idea for a new project. I did a few doodles. I remembered the false teeth. I did an eye with legs, but it looked gross. I did a pair of lips that were really a sofa, but I've seen that before somewhere so it wasn't really my idea. Then I designed a pair of earrings shaped like lavatories.

But I just couldn't get going with it, somehow, and in the end I drifted away and started watching TV again. The only thing that cheered me up was the thought of those clockwork false teeth.

Next day Yasmin brought them to school! Oh bliss! Oh joy! She made them walk across Mrs Jenkins' desk, and even Mrs Jenkins laughed properly out loud, not just her usual tight-lipped smile.

At break Yasmin drew a huge crowd as her teeth marched up and down, chomping from time to time. Max seemed a bit embarrassed that Yasmin loved his present so much. He almost looked as if he wished that somebody else had bought them.

'I've decided I'm going to give my teeth a name,' said Yasmin at lunchtime. 'I'm going to call them Gnasher.'

'They're so cool!' I sighed. 'They're the funniest thing I've ever seen. I was trying to describe them to my mum yesterday but she just couldn't imagine what I was talking about.'

'Borrow them if you like, Ruby,' said Yasmin.

'Really? Really and truly? Could I?' I was thrilled at the idea. Joe was going to love them.

'Of course!' grinned Yasmin. 'Only take good care of them, OK? Because if you don't, they'll tell me afterwards.'

'I promise,' I said. 'I'll give Gnasher the best time he's ever had.'

'Fine,' said Yasmin. 'Gnasher, you can go home

with Auntie Ruby.' She wound the teeth up again
and they started chattering and strutting about on
the dinner table. The dinner lady came up.

'Put that thing away, Yasmin,' she said, 'or I
might have to take it off you.'

Yasmin quickly put Gnasher away safely in her
pocket. 'I hate that dinner lady,' she whispered.
'And once I've got the hang of my magic kit I'm
going to put a spell on her.'

At home time, Yasmin handed Gnasher over.
She even kissed him goodbye. There were just so
many jokes you could invent from a set of false
teeth. I made Gnasher say 'Goodbye, Mummy!' to
Yasmin. He promised to be good.

I walked home very fast, holding the teeth safe

in my pocket. I couldn't wait to show them to Mum and Dad. And Joe would love them, of course. When I got home, Mum's car was parked outside. Great! I could show her the teeth right away. I got them out of my pocket, and ran up the path.

Then – disaster! I tripped over my own feet and went crashing down on to the path. The teeth hit the stone with a horrible noise of cracking plastic, and I completed the job by falling heavily on them with a sickening final crunch.

I sat up and picked up the teeth. They were twisted and wrong. You couldn't even turn the key any more. I had wrecked Yasmin's star teeth. I had ruined her most famous present, which had even made our stony-faced teacher laugh. I had killed Gnasher. There was only one thing to do: cry.

CHAPTER 6

It's not the end
of the world

'RUBY! What's the matter?' Mum came rushing out of the kitchen, holding a wooden spoon.

I showed her the teeth. They were totally trashed.

'Oh dear!' she winced. 'Still, maybe Joe can fix them. He's brilliant at mending things, isn't he, love? Stop crying, now, it's not the end of the world.'

Huh! What did she know? Of course it was the

end of the world. I trudged upstairs to Joe's bedroom and knocked on the door.

'Come!' he called in a mock posh voice. I wasn't in the mood for Joe's jokes, but I needed his help. I went in.

Joe was sitting at his work table, making something out of small pieces of wood and wire. He makes models – well, sculptures, really. He even had an exhibition once – at Holly's mum's gallery. I was hoping he and Holly might get together then, but somehow it didn't happen.

'Joe! I've broken Yasmin's teeth!'

'Smart move. I always hated that overbite. Don't worry, she can always grow a new set, like a shark.'

He could see I'd been crying, but he still couldn't help making stupid jokes. But maybe he was making stupid jokes *because* he could see I'd been crying. I had to be patient and not get riled.

I just handed him the teeth. He looked at them, turning them over in his hands. Joe has nice hands, though his feet smell terrible.

'I can't do anything with this,' he said. 'What did you do to it?'

'I fell on it,' I said.

'We should hire you out to builders,' said Joe. 'If a factory needed demolishing, you could fall on it.'

'Can't you do anything?' I begged.

'Look, the plastic's smashed,' said Joe. 'Plus the winding mechanism's crushed and bent. The only thing to do with this is throw it away.'

My eyes filled with tears again. They made everything look weird. Joe's room, and Joe, suddenly bulged and slanted. It was like looking into an aquarium.

'Don't start that infernal caterwauling,' he said. 'These teeth are just junk anyway.'

'But they're Yasmin's!' I explained. 'It was her favourite birthday present! She's only lent them to me! She'll kill me.'

'Well, that would solve a major problem of

ours,' said Joe. But he got up and reached for his notebook. 'I wonder if she'd kill you in a special Turkish way. Schoolgirl Kills Friend with Overdose of Turkish Delight. "She Went with a Smile on Her Face," Says Grieving Family.'

Joe went online and did a search on clockwork teeth. There were loads of teeth that you could wind up and they would chatter, but we couldn't see a single set of teeth with legs that walked about.

'You could get her the chattering teeth,' said Joe.

'I can't!' I said, cringing at the thought. 'I have to replace them with an exact same set! She mustn't know I've broken them!'

'Are you scared of her or something?' Joe suddenly looked round, straight into my eyes, puzzled. 'She's only a little kid, for God's sake.'

'Yasmin can be really fierce and frightening,' I told him. 'She loves rows. She's got a terrible violent temper.'

'Well, serve you right for a bad choice of friends,' said Joe, turning back to his notebook. He was surfing the web for his own sake now. I saw him do a search on images of harps.

'What are you making?' I asked him.

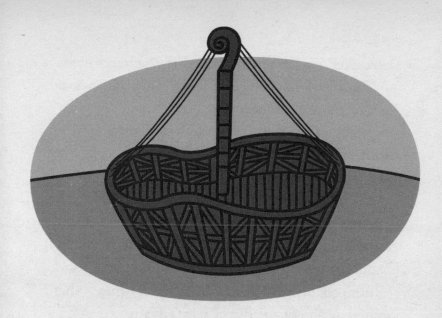

'Musical instruments that can fly,' he said. 'Or amphibious ones that can go on water. The cello-boat is my latest.'

He pointed to a small sculpture on the window sill. You could tell he'd just varnished it or something. It was drying. The shape of the boat was exactly like a tiny cello, but sort of opened up, without its front. The bit with the strings and fingerboard were set in the boat pointing straight up, like a mast with ropes and stuff.

'It's amazing!' I said.

Joe shrugged. 'I'm working on the harp now,' he told me. 'But I'm not getting anywhere.' He was studying pictures of harps. 'I mean, what do they look like?' He frowned. I stared at the harps.

'They look like angels,' I said. 'With their wings sort of folded behind them.'

'Right! That'll do!' said Joe suddenly. 'You've outlived your usefulness. Get the hell out of here, and take your busted teeth with you.'

On the way downstairs I started to feel bad again. The teeth were broken. I would have to tell Yasmin tomorrow. The thought made me sick with guilt.

As I entered the kitchen, the phone rang. I sort of jumped, because I thought it was Yasmin – that somehow she *knew*. But it was Tiffany.

'Hi, Ruby,' she said, trying to sound posh and businesslike so I wouldn't think she was ringing to beg Joe to get back with her. 'Is Joe in?'

'No, sorry,' I said. 'I don't know where he is. Can I take a message?'

'No,' said Tiffany, trying to sound tremendously light-hearted about the whole thing, even though her heart was probably breaking, 'it's not important. Cheers, Rube!'

She rang off breezily, possibly to plunge her head in her pillow and sob for hours. Although I don't like Tiffany and I'm thrilled that she and Joe have split up, I can't help feeling a tiny bit sorry for her sometimes.

Joe has written a notice and stuck it on the fridge door: *IF TIFFANY RINGS, I AM OUT.* I had obeyed this order four times already.

'Tiffany?' said Mum. I nodded. She sighed and shook her head. 'I hope you don't have boyfriends till you go to college,' she said. 'I can't stand all this drama.'

'I'm not going to have boyfriends ever!' I snapped. 'And I'm not even going to have friends, now, because Joe can't mend Yasmin's teeth and we can't find anything like them on the internet.'

'We could have a look in town on Saturday,' said Mum. 'But that's another four days.'

My heart sank. Though there was a lovely smell of cheese and potato pie, I felt too sick to even think about food.

'I'll have to try and stall her till the weekend, then,' I said. I knew it would be hopeless. Yasmin is very good at telling when I'm lying.

'You could just come clean and confess all tomorrow morning,' said Mum.

'No way!' I shrieked. 'I'd be dead meat!'

'I hate that phrase,' said Mum, wrinkling her nose. 'If I ever hear you saying it again, I shall become a vegetarian and there will be no more sausages in this house, ever.'

At suppertime I managed to eat a bit of cheese and potato pie, but I had to think very hard about *The Simpsons* to avoid that guilty sinking feeling. Getting to sleep was hard too. I tried thinking about angels looking like harps, and angels playing harps, and wondering if heaven was really like that, and if it's true that angels aren't male or female, just beings. There's a boy at Joe's school who's a bit like that. He's soooo cool. He has shoulder-length golden curls and his name is Seth Phillips.

Next day I was so nervous I could hardly walk. Mum delivered me at the school gate and I kind of tottered forward like a rag doll trying to walk. I could see Yasmin in the middle of the yard and she was looking at me. But there was something really odd about her face. She looked – well, different. A horrid cold spear of terror sliced through my heart. She knew! She *knew*! I've often thought Yasmin was psychic and this was the proof.

CHAPTER 7
Let me in!

I WALKED TOWARDS Yasmin, trying to smile. Well, I couldn't just avoid her, could I? We hadn't had a row or anything. Yet.

'Hi, Yas!' I said, trying to sound friendly and breezy.

'Hi, Rube!' she grinned – but her grin seemed a tiny bit empty somehow. Maybe I was imagining it because I was feeling so guilty.

We linked arms and strolled across the yard. Nobody said anything. Usually it's a competition as to who can talk most. I had to say something totally unconnected with Yasmin's false teeth. My mind was in a spin, though. Everything I said seemed to lead straight to teeth.

I wish I was allowed to have a dog. With sharp teeth, obviously. *How are you feeling today, Yasmin?* Fine, apart from the toothache. *I wonder what it'll be for lunch today.* Free-range chicken – just like those free-range teeth.

'We're going away this weekend,' said Yasmin suddenly.

'Oh, nice,' I said, relieved that one of us had managed to say something. 'Where?'

'We're going to London,' said Yasmin. And she blushed. That was weird. 'So I'm afraid I won't be around, Ruby.'

'That's OK!' I said.

'I was hoping you'd be able to come round to my house, but we'll be away,' said Yasmin. 'Sorry.'

She looked strange. As if she was not quite sure about something. Yasmin doesn't normally look like that. Normally she's bouncy and confident. She doesn't ever look kind of mysterious. Well, she didn't ever until now.

I smiled and pretended to hum to show I was totally fine about it. But inside I was terrified. Yasmin knew! She knew I'd broken her clockwork teeth! She was psychic! Telepathic! She could read my mind! I went on humming, but it didn't sound too good.

Froggo ran up to us. Thank goodness! We needed rescuing from something, although I wasn't sure quite what.

'Mount Olympus Mons on Mars is three times the size of Mount Everest!' said Froggo. Boys are like that. They spend hours memorising curious facts and useless statistics. They don't do relationships.

'I wouldn't want to go to Mars,' I said. 'It sounds a bit hot.'

'I'm going there for my hols,' said Froggo. 'My

dad is going to play darts in the Mars Bars. Ha ha!'
And he ran off. Although this wasn't exactly conversation, it filled the time nicely until the bell
went.

I had decided not to mention the teeth. I would
wait and see if Yasmin mentioned them. If she
didn't, it was proof that she knew that I'd broken
them – although that wasn't Yasmin's usual way
of going about things. Usually she'd yell something
like, 'You've broken my teeth, you sad loser!' And
wallop me with her schoolbag.

But nothing like that happened all day. Yasmin
spent time with me, but she was a bit distant and
polite. Luckily Hannah was there a lot of the time,
and she was moaning about her TV breaking down.
Lauren was there too. She was excited because one
of her sheepdogs was about to have puppies.
Lauren's life is so amazing. I wish I was her.

When we were with Lauren and Hannah,
Yasmin seemed fine. But when we were alone
together, it was as if we'd only just met. It didn't
feel like being best mates at all. I was worried sick.
But still I waited. If she didn't say anything about
the teeth, maybe I would have to mention them at
the end of school. Maybe I could pretend I'd forgotten them.

Or maybe I should ask her if I could keep them a bit longer? To show to somebody I was going to see at the weekend? This was a better idea. I'd be able to tell by Yasmin's reaction if she suspected me of breaking the teeth or not. And it would give me more time to try and find a replacement.

I waited till the very last minute, when we were walking across the yard. Yasmin's mum was waiting by the gate. My mum wasn't – thank goodness. I was sure she'd have blurted out something about the broken teeth.

'Oh, Yasmin!' I gasped in a dramatic way, as if I'd just remembered. 'Your teeth!' Yasmin looked blankly at me.

'My teeth?' she asked.

'Your clockwork teeth you lent me!' I said. 'I meant to ask you, could I keep them till the weekend to show them to my cousin?'

'Yes, sure, keep them as long as you like,' said Yasmin. We were at the gate now. She didn't look suspicious. But she did look a bit odd.

'Hi, Ruby!' said Yasmin's mum. 'Want a lift home? Or maybe you'd like to come back to our house for tea?'

I noticed Yasmin look quickly at her mum in a frantic kind of way, as if to say, *No, Mum, no way!* Normally, of course, she'd be pulling me into the car.

'Thanks, but I can't, I'm sorry,' I said. 'I told Joe I'd meet him at the Dolphin Cafe and we'd walk home together.'

Yasmin looked hugely relieved. She obviously didn't want any more of my company today. Well, you wouldn't, would you? I'd broken her star toy.

I walked home sadly on my own. It had been a lie about Joe waiting for me at the Dolphin Cafe. It had been a lie about my cousin. My only cousins are in Australia. Yasmin knows that, but she hadn't picked up on it. She so obviously had things on her mind. But how had she found out about the teeth?

As I passed the Dolphin Cafe, I saw teenagers inside laughing and joking. Some were sitting at tables outside on the pavement. They were talking on their mobile phones. That must be it! Suddenly I realised. Joe must have talked to somebody last night – he spends ages texting and talking to people late at night.

He'd told somebody about my breaking Yasmin's teeth, and they'd told Yasmin's big sister Zerrin! My whole body felt suddenly cold. Info travels like the speed of light on the teenage grapevine. I would kill Joe for this when I got home.

But when I did get home he wasn't there. Nobody was home yet, except – as I turned in at our gate, my heart gave a horrid little leap – Tiffany was sitting on the doorstep. When she saw me, she kind of lurched to her feet.

'Ruby!' she said. 'Let me in! I gotta see Joe!'

She grabbed me. I could smell her breath. Ohmigawd! It smelt of alcohol! I was going to be home alone with a drunk teenager! What could I do? Joe would kill me if I let her in to wait for him. But what choice did I have?

CHAPTER 8
Help me, Ruby!

'I CAN'T LET you in,' I said. 'Sorry.'

'Why not?' yelled Tiffany. 'I've been in your house hundreds of times. Your mum thinks I'm cool!' This was *so* not true.

'I'm sorry!' I said. 'I can't let you in because . . . I've lost my key.'

'I can see it in your hand, Rube!' shouted Tiffany. She put her arm round me and gave me a horrible alcoholic hug. 'Don't be horrid!' she pleaded. 'I love you, Ruby. I love you, I love you, I love you. You're the little sister I always dreamed of.'

She was the big sister I'd always had nightmares about – but I couldn't tell her that. Although she was a little bit drunk, she was still a lot stronger than me. She got hold of my hand and prised my fingers apart. I was going to have to let her in. Apart from anything else, I was dying for a pee.

'OK, then,' I said. 'Get off! I'll open the door.' She let go of me. I hate the fact that big people can force you to do things, just because they're stronger. It isn't fair. 'But Joe won't want to talk to you when he gets back. There's a notice by the phone in the kitchen that says *IF TIFFANY RINGS, I AM OUT.*'

'He's so cruel!' wailed Tiffany.

I opened the door and she pushed past me. I know when people drink too much they behave badly. And Tiffany never has good manners even when she's sober.

'I don't want to speak to him anyway!' she said, heading for the kitchen. 'Let me see that notice! And gimme a glass of water!'

'Help yourself!' I said.

'Wait!' Tiffany was halfway to the kitchen, but she stopped and looked as if she was thinking, hard. 'I want my cards! I sent him loadsa cards! I want them back!'

In a flash I realised she was planning to go upstairs and ransack his room. I knew his latest sculptures would be set out on the table and the window sills, drying. Tiffany would trash his work in a fit of rage! I'd done it once myself and I still hate myself for it.

I had to save Joe's sculptures. I turned and raced upstairs. Being small and monkeyish, and not drunk, I got up there before Tiffany, who was finding the stairs a bit of a puzzle. I ran into Joe's bedroom and locked the door.

Thank goodness his room had a lock! Moments later Tiffany arrived outside and started hammering on the door.

'Lemme in!' she yelled. 'Lemme in, Ruby! I won't touch anything! I just want my cards! Help me, Ruby! Don't be so horrid!' My heart was pounding.

'Listen!' I said, but she interrupted me.

'I love you, Ruby! I love you! Be nice to me! Let me in!'

'Listen!' I said again. 'I'll look for the cards for you. You go downstairs and wait in the sitting room. Watch a DVD or something. I'll bring them down to you.'

'They're private!' she groaned. 'Private!'

'I won't read them,' I said. 'I'll just look for them!'

'No, no!' she wailed. 'Let me in! Don't be so horrible!' And she started hammering on the door again.

I didn't move. I hardly dared breathe. I prayed for Mum or Dad to come home. Or even better, Joe. This was his mess after all.

'Ruby!' There was a slithering sound, as if Tiffany had sunk to her knees and was now slumped against the door. I heard a scratching noise. 'Let me in! I'll give you a sweetie!'

'I don't like sweets,' I said, trying to sound hard. It was a lie, of course. I haven't got a sweet tooth like Yasmin, but I do like chocolates. And sherbert lemons.

Oh no! The thought of Yasmin's sweet tooth had reminded me of my own problems. But the broken teeth were nothing compared to my urgent need to visit the loo. Wildly, I looked around Joe's room. There was just nothing like a toilet or a potty in there. I was beginning to think I'd have to stick my bum out of the window and pee into the garden, when, thank God, I heard the front door slam.

'Joe!' Tiffany roared. I heard feet thundering up the stairs. 'Ruby won't let me in!' she wailed. 'I only want my cards!'

'Ruby!' This was Joe hammering at the door now. I unlocked it and raced past them into the bathroom. Just in time.

I stayed in the bathroom for ages, because Joe and Tiffany were having a shouting match. I put my fingers in my ears. They were saying terrible things to each other, and there was a lot of swearing. I'm definitely not going to have a boyfriend, ever. It's fine in the early stages when it's all lovey-dovey (although even that can be a sickening sight to younger bros and sisters) – but when the big break-up comes, it's horrendous.

After a while I heard the front door slam again. This time it was Mum arriving home. Joe and Tiffany's terrible row stopped immediately. There was the sound of footsteps going downstairs, voices in the hall (but quiet ones – including Mum's) and then the front door banged again. Then it was peaceful again.

I came out of the bathroom and met Joe, who was heading back to his room. He looked very red in the face, but he wasn't crying this time, thank goodness. Once before, when he and Tiffany had a row, I saw him crying. That was ages ago, at Halloween. They've broken up loads of times. But this time it's for keeps. I can tell.

'I was scared she was going to break your sculptures,' I said.

'Oh really?' said Joe in a very snarly voice. 'I thought that was your job.' And he went into his room and slammed the door.

I was furious. So that was all the thanks I got for heroically defending his sculpture thingies! The beast!

'Well, thanks for your appreciation!' I yelled. 'And thanks for telling everybody about the broken teeth, too! You landed me right in it, slimeball!'

Joe's door flew open. He glared out at me, but

he spoke very softly. It was really scary for a moment.

'I didn't tell anybody about your stupid teeth!' he hissed. 'Now push off and leave me in peace!'

I went downstairs. Mum was unpacking some groceries. She looked a bit embarrassed because of the Tiffany episode.

'Tiffany forced me to let her in,' I said. 'She practically ripped the key out of my hand. She was drunk.'

'Never mind, sweetheart,' she said soothingly. 'Apart from that, how was the rest of your day?' And she gave me a hopeful smile. Mum is such an optimist. It's really annoying sometimes.

CHAPTER 9
You started this!

NEXT DAY AT school, Yasmin was just the same – strange and a bit formal, as if she had something on her mind.

'What are you going to see in London?' I asked her at break. It would be good to talk about her trip to London, because it had nothing to do with teeth.

But Yasmin didn't look pleased at the chance to make me jealous with her wonderful weekend. Last time she went to London, she and her sister had an amazing shopping trip, then at night they went to see a show. And they stayed in a beautiful hotel looking out on to a park.

Now Yasmin was looking thoughtful, though. She didn't answer for a few moments. I waited.

'Don't mention my trip to London to anybody,' she whispered. 'It's supposed to be a secret.'

I was puzzled.

'What do you mean, a secret?' I asked. 'Who would mind you going to London?'

Yasmin's eyes flashed in annoyance.

'Nobody would mind, Ruby!' she snapped. 'It's just supposed to be a secret, OK? Plus it's nobody else's business. I only told you because you're my best mate. I don't want you going around gossiping about it all the time.'

'I wasn't going to go round gossiping about it!' I hissed. 'I was just talking, that's all. I've never gossipated about you!' That was stupid. I hadn't meant to say 'gossipated'. It came out all wrong. I hate the way when you're trying to be dignified and cross you sometimes say something stupid.

'You so *have*!' Yasmin was getting going now. She loves a row. She was going to have one whether I wanted to or not.

'I have not!' I yelled. Usually I hate rows, but the way Yasmin was behaving at the moment, it would almost be a relief to have a proper row to clear the air.

'You told Holly I'd got a temper!' stormed Yasmin.

'Well, you have got a temper!' I shouted back. 'Look at you now!'

'I have so NOT got a temper! You're the one with the temper! You started this!'

'I didn't! You liar!'

'Don't call me a liar! You started this, Ruby!'

'How? How? How did I start this?'

'Trying to find out all about my trip to London when it's none of your business!'

'I was just trying to make conversation because you're so moody and weird these days! I don't think you even want to be my friend any more!'

'Well, you're right there!' Yasmin exploded. 'I don't want to be your stupid friend. So you can go and take a running jump!'

Yasmin turned round and strode off. I just stood there. I was shocked. Yasmin and I have had loads of rows, but this one felt a bit more serious. I felt sick. I felt like crying. But it wasn't going to help, being sick or crying. I mustn't let Yasmin see she'd upset me at all. I strolled towards Froggo, trying to look casual.

'What's your latest amazing fact?' I asked him.

'Turtles can breathe through their bottoms,' he told me. This distracted me for a minute.

'Well, anybody can breathe *out* through their bottoms,' I said. 'It's breathing *in* that's tricky.'

Froggo laughed. Phew! It was such a relief being with a boy after all that emotion and stress. 'Tell me another stupid stat,' I said.

'You can tell the sex of a turtle by the sound it makes,' he said. 'A male grunts, a female hisses.' This was interesting, and made me want to go off right away and play with some turtles, but it wasn't quite as funny as Froggo's first bizarre fact. I didn't manage to laugh. In a way it's awful having a terrific joke and then trying to equal it. It leaves you feeling slightly down.

'Froggo,' I said, 'if you'd broken something belonging to somebody else, what would you do?'

'I'd blame you!' grinned Froggo, and he ran off. This wasn't much help. It had been stupid to ask a boy something like that.

For the rest of the day Yasmin sulked. She sat at the other side of the room with Hannah. I sat by the window with Lauren. That's what usually happens when we have a bust-up.

'Do you want me to tell Yasmin you're sorry?' whispered Lauren at lunchtime.

'No, I don't!' I snapped. 'I'm not sorry! I haven't done anything wrong!' Lauren looked a bit nervous. She hates rows even more than I do. 'Thanks, though,' I said. 'Thank goodness you haven't got a foul temper like Yasmin. At least you and I will never have a row.'

Lauren looked pleased for a while. We were queuing for lunch. Yasmin and Hannah were way up ahead. They had pushed in, but they'd got away with it.

I was feeling dismal again. When I'd told Lauren that I didn't want to get back together with Yasmin and I hadn't done anything wrong, that was not quite true. First, I did want to get back with her. Second, I had done something wrong. I'd broken her star present, killed her beloved Gnasher. What could be worse than that?

'Ruby,' said Lauren anxiously, 'do you think people who haven't got a temper are boring?' Poor old Lauren! Worrying that she was dull!

'No, no!' I insisted, squeezing her arm. 'I hate shouting and rows. People who don't like shouting are the best people in the world.'

Lauren looked relieved. I felt relieved. When we

got up to the food counter, though, all the pizza had gone and we had to have risotto.

Hannah and Yasmin had got pizza, and they were sitting with Froggo and Max. Yasmin gave me a triumphant glance which seemed to say, *I've got it all: the pizza and the boys!* I ignored her.

Lauren and I had to sit with a rather smelly girl called Nadia and her friend Jules, who does horrible deafening shrieks of laughter which give me a headache.

So it wasn't a very good lunchtime, really. The afternoon was pure hell too. Mrs Jenkins caught me not listening and told me off in front of the whole class.

By the time I started to walk home, I was really fed up. But I heard somebody say, 'Hey, Ruby! Wait for me!' I turned round. It was Holly.

'How did Yasmin's party go?' she asked. 'What present did you give her?'

As we walked along, I told Holly the whole story. She listened carefully.

'And I don't think we're ever going to be friends again,' I said, 'because even if we do make it up, as soon as she finds out I've broken Gnasher, she'll be furious with me again.'

'Where did she get the teeth?' asked Holly.

'Uh – they were a present from, um, Max, I think.' I racked my brains, trying to remember.

'Well, ask Max where he got them. Then you'll know how to get your hands on a replacement!' said Holly breezily.

No way! She was so clever. This idea was going to save my friendship, I was sure – possibly even my life.

I hate it when you say that!

I RANG MAX. I had worked out what to say. Obviously I wouldn't tell him I'd broken his present to Yasmin. He would be cross, and he'd be sure to tell everybody at school tomorrow. So I just said, kind of casually, 'Oh, Max, you know those cool clockwork teeth you gave Yasmin? Can you tell me where you got them, because I want to get some for my cousin.'

The imaginary cousin again. She (or he) was playing quite a big part in my life these days.

'Oh, right,' said Max. 'Well, sorry, but my dad

brought them back from Hong Kong. I think he got them in a market or something.'

My heart sank. Moments ago I had been so sure I'd be able to find out where the teeth came from. And now I was back to square one. I just had to find a set of teeth that were *exactly the same* as Gnasher. I couldn't face telling Yasmin I'd broken them. She was already furious with me. She was probably already writing poisonous things about me – in the secret book I'd given her.

I didn't eat much supper. The atmosphere was slightly gloomy anyway. The sun had gone in and heavy dark clouds hung over the street outside. Mum sighed.

'I miss my lovely tree,' she said. 'Do you think the council will plant a new one in its place?'

'If they can afford it,' said Dad. 'I don't expect they can, though. The councillors will have spent all our council tax on freebies to study public transport in the French Riviera.'

'I wish we could go to the French Riviera,' sighed Mum. 'They've got lovely trees there. They've got those lovely mimosas that bloom in February.'

'You'd probably get your handbag snatched,' said Dad with a cheery grin.

Mum looked grumpy. Joe got up from his chair. He hadn't said a thing all evening.

'*Excuse me*, Joe, if you please!' snapped Mum. He grunted something and went off upstairs. 'He's left his dirty plate on the table again!' said Mum. She sighed for a third time.

'It is our turn to clear the table, Mum,' I reminded her.

We've got a new system in our house. There's the women's team, that's Mum and me, and the men's team – Dad and Joe, obviously. We take it in turns to clear the table and load the dishwasher. But Mum still does most of the cooking. Although Dad cooks during the school hols, because being a teacher, he has a lot more time off than Mum.

'Can we go into town and look for the clock-work teeth on Saturday?' I asked. 'Because Yasmin and I have already had a row and she doesn't even know I've broken her teeth yet. She'll kill me when she finds out.'

'Oh, do stop fussing about those teeth, Ruby,' said Mum, looking irritated.

'Please can we go to town, though?' I went on. 'You *promised!*'

'I hate it when you say that!' snapped Mum. 'I didn't actually *promise*, as a matter of fact. And all sort of things could happen which would mean I'd have to change my plans. But at the moment, yes, I am planning to take you round the shops to look for Yasmin's blinking teeth, but if you nag me any more about it, you can forget it!'

She got up in a strop and flounced out to the kitchen. Dad and I exchanged looks. He raised his fingers to his lips and started very quietly and gently to clear the table, even though it was really the turn of the women's team.

And then the doorbell rang. We froze.

'See who that is, Brian, please!' called Mum from the kitchen. 'I've had enough of dealing with that blasted Tiffany!'

I cringed in case it was Tiffany on the doorstep. She might have heard Mum describe her as 'that blasted Tiffany'.

I raced to the window and peeped out. It wasn't Tiffany. I saw Uncle Tristram's car parked out in the road. His car is totally cool. It's an old red sports car, although he never goes fast in it.

'It's Uncle Tristram!' I yelled in glee. I was pleased because he's always good fun. Maybe his girlfriend, Astrid, would be with him, too. She's tall and Dutch and incredibly cool and stylish.

I rushed to the door. Dad was following me. We opened it with beaming smiles, eager to see Uncle Tristram's cute grin. He was going to rescue us from our gloomy evening.

But the moment we saw him, we realised something was wrong.

'Hi, Bruv,' he said to Dad in a kind of mock *Eastenders* voice. 'I was at a loose end so I thought I'd drop round. Hi, Ruby!'

'Come in!' grinned Dad.

Tristram came in and hugged me, and then he hugged Dad too.

'No Astrid today?' asked Dad, leading the way into the sitting room.

'No Astrid today,' said Tristram. 'And, to be

honest, no Astrid from now on, unfortunately. She's run off with a Polish plasterer.'

'No!' said Dad, shocked. 'Hard luck!'

'I probably deserve it,' said Tristram sadly. 'I am very boring, I know.'

'Nonsense!' said Dad. 'You're not as boring as me. You work in a bookshop. You've got long hair. You've got a sports car. What more could any woman want?'

Tristram shrugged. 'There I was,' he went on, sitting down on our sofa and leaning back as if he was very, very tired, 'planning to redecorate the sitting room. I got this bloke in because he seemed very reasonable and hard-working. I've got no complaints about the plastering – it was first rate – but running off with Astrid wasn't in the original work schedule.'

At this point Mum came in and Tristram told the whole story again, with a lot more detail. At one point Mum said, 'Ruby, haven't you got any homework to do?' She didn't want me to hear all the sordid details of my uncle's bust-up. But I'd done my homework, so she didn't really have an excuse to send me out. Anyway, Tristram wasn't crying or swearing or anything. He just seemed a bit low.

'I've got to choose the paint without her now,' he said in a depressed voice. 'I'm torn between Blue Ashes and Smoke Blue.'

'Why not yellow?' said Dad, trying to jolly things along. 'It's, you know, more cheerful.'

'She liked blue,' said Tristram. 'I'll paint it in memory of her. And if she comes back, she'll be pleased. Yes, she liked blue . . . the Polish chap had bright blue eyes. I think that's what swung it.'

'But your eyes are blue, Tristram!' said Mum. He shook his head sadly.

'No, no,' he said. 'Mine are grey. That's what it says on my passport.'

That was a kind of important detail that seemed to clinch it, apparently. After that Dad took Tristram out for a drink, and I went up to my tree house for a think. Suddenly there was a flash of lightning and it started to rain really hard. All these storms! Everything was rubbish at the moment. Even the weather.

Uncle Tristram had split up with lovely Astrid. Joe and Tiffany were finished. Holly and Dom were history. Our tree had gone for ever. And Yasmin was already in a rage with me, although this was nothing compared to the fury that she would unleash as soon as she knew I had killed Gnasher.

CHAPTER 11
She's got a
gold star for sulking

UNCLE TRISTRAM stayed the night, and next morning he drove me to school in his little red sports car. It had stopped raining, so we had the roof down.

'Let's have some jazz,' said Uncle Tristram. He switched on the CD player and some jolly music started to play. 'Jelly Roll Morton and his Red Hot Peppers,' he said proudly. 'Wonderful jazz recorded eighty years ago.'

I was feeling a hundred times better already,

with the wind in my hair and the sun on my shoulders. Uncle Tristram drives quite slowly and sensibly, so I wasn't scared.

'This is like going on holiday,' I said. 'I wish you could drive me to school every day.'

'I wish I could too,' said Uncle Tris. 'But that's a great idea – a holiday. I think I might go to Paris for a few days.'

'Paris!' I yelled. 'Wow! Wish I could come!'

'I was planning to go to Paris when I first met Astrid,' said Uncle Tristram. 'And she would never go, because she'd been mugged there twice in the past. But now I'm free I can do what I like.'

'I'm never going to have a boyfriend or get married,' I told him.

'Very sensible,' he agreed. 'I'm not going to bother with women from now on. I might get a dog instead.'

'Oh, yes! I've always wanted a dog, but Mum says it's not fair because everybody's out all day.'

'Hmmm, she's right, of course. But next time you come to stay with me, you can come and help me choose a dog from the animal rescue pound.'

I almost threw my arms around Uncle Tristram right then, I was so thrilled. However, I know it's very important never to distract the driver,

because Mum always goes on and on about it, so I waited till we got to school.

'Thanks so much for bringing me!' I said, giving him a huge hug. 'Everybody will be so jealous! I hope you have a great time in Paris! And when you come back we can choose your dog!'

'Thanks for cheering me up, Rube!' said Uncle Tris. 'I feel terrific now. So many exciting plans!'

As I walked into the schoolyard, Froggo ran up. 'Cool car!' he yelled. 'Who's that? He looks like a film star.'

'It's my uncle,' I said rather grandly. 'He's just off to Paris to cheer himself up after a messy divorce.' It wasn't really a divorce, because Tristram and Astrid hadn't been married. But it sounded better that way.

'I might live in Paris when I grow up,' said Froggo. 'Or LA. Or possibly Monaco, because of the Grand Prix. Where are you going to live?'

'In the rainforest,' I said. 'I don't like cities.' I was glad that I knew exactly where I wanted to be in future. Even some grown-ups don't seem to know what they want to do or where they want to go. Uncle Tristram is a bit like that.

'My auntie Astrid ran off with somebody else,' I told Froggo.

'What?' asked Froggo. 'Your aunt Asteroid?'

We joked around for a few minutes. Suddenly I saw Yasmin out of the corner of my eye, over by the tree. She was watching me, but pretending not to. I had the sinking feeling again. I'd felt heaps better with Uncle Tristram, and it was good talking to Froggo, but I hadn't escaped from my Yasmin dilemma.

Lauren came up. 'Have you made it up with Yasmin yet?' she asked. I wished she could have said something about Uncle Tristram and his amazing red sports car, but maybe Lauren hadn't noticed us arriving.

'No, Yasmin and I are still not speaking,' I sighed. 'She's got a gold star for sulking so it may go on for weeks.'

Yasmin was still not speaking to me at lunchtime. I ignored her. I was determined not to speak first either. OK, I had broken her teeth, but apart from that she was clearly in the wrong. And she didn't even know about the teeth yet. She'd just yelled at me and caused the row in the first place.

Geography was last lesson: Improving the Environment. Mrs Jenkins showed us a picture of some polar bears standing on an iceberg that had

melted almost totally away. They looked kind of puzzled. The iceberg was all thin and wobbly as if it might topple over at any moment. One or two people giggled.

'It's not funny,' said Mrs Jenkins. She didn't say it snappily, but sadly. 'Global warming means the ice is melting around the North Pole. So the polar bears' home is vanishing. In fifty years' time, maybe sooner, there may not be any polar bears left alive.'

I felt shocked and sick. Poor polar bears! How could we do this to them?

'We can already see how global warming is

affecting us,' Mrs Jenkins went on. 'That storm last weekend, for instance.'

I thought of our lovely tree, and how I missed it. I know it hadn't actually been *our* tree, it had just been one of the trees that line our street, but it had felt like ours.

'Global warming will mean many more storms and floods and devastation,' said Mrs Jenkins. 'People living in low-lying areas by the sea might have their houses swept away.'

I wondered if our house was in a low-lying area. I hoped not. It all sounded terribly dangerous.

'There are ways in which we can reduce the amount of carbon dioxide we produce,' said Mrs Jenkins, sounding a bit more hopeful. 'Does anyone have any ideas?'

I was still a bit unsure of what carbon dioxide was exactly, but a lot of people already knew loads about this. Froggo especially. He's a bit of an eco-freak.

'There are hybrid cars,' he said, 'that run on electricity and petrol! The Toyota Prius. They're brilliant, because you can still go fast in them on motorways and stuff, and when you're on the motorway it charges up the battery, and then when you get into a town and have to drive slowly again, the engine switches over to electricity.'

Other people had various ideas and Mrs Jenkins explained the whole thing. Apparently we have to turn the central heating down, ride a bike instead of using the car, not eat food that's been flown in from hundreds of miles away, that sort of thing. Our homework was to design a poster to make people aware of how they could help to reduce global warming.

'I want this homework in on Monday,' said Mrs Jenkins. 'The ten best posters will be displayed on the school website, and then we'll vote for the very best one. It'll be printed and we'll distribute it to everybody to raise awareness.'

I knew my dad would be interested in all this because he's a geography teacher. Maybe he could help me with my poster. He's got loads of books and magazines and stuff in his study. And he knows all the best eco websites. I was sort of excited about the idea of designing a poster. I hadn't done any art since I'd been working on Yasmin's card.

I looked across the room to see if she would smile. I caught her eye for an instant, but she looked away with a cross face. I would have to wait until Monday to try to make it up with her

now, because she was going to London this week-end. It was handy actually, as it gave me a chance to find a pair of teeth exactly like the ones I'd broken.

Uncle Tristram had promised to keep an eye open in Bath, where he lives. It's a big city with lots of interesting and weird shops. And, of course, Mum was going to take me round our shops, too, although it all seemed a bit unimportant now compared to the polar bears.

CHAPTER 12

I want to kill them

WHEN I GOT HOME I told Dad all about our Improving the Environment lesson. He listened carefully. He didn't just make jokes like he does sometimes.

'It's frightening,' I said. 'What if the earth just gets hotter and hotter and kind of burns up? What about the monkeys?'

'It won't get that bad,' Dad promised me. 'I think everybody's got the message now. Not like twenty years ago when we eco-warriors were warning about this and nobody was listening.'

I've seen photos of Dad in his Greenpeace days. He's got long hair and a beard. I think in a way he looks younger now than he did then.

'But what if we've broken the planet?' I asked. 'What if it's totally trashed? I hate those people who wouldn't listen. I want to kill them.'

'Ruby, that wouldn't help.'

'Yes, it would!' I was ready to kill them all myself.

'Listen, if you design a really brilliant poster, it might help to get the message across. So let's get the paints out, shall we?'

Dad sat with me and pretended to help, though he was really watching the cricket on TV out of the corner of his eye. I drew a picture of the earth going up in flames. Joe walked in and looked at my work.

'Hmm,' he said. 'Nice Christmas pudding!' I hit him, not hard, because he moved away and it's hard to hit somebody when you're sitting down unless they co-operate.

My drawing of the earth did look a bit like a Christmas pudding, though, I had to admit. I started again. I drew some trees that were dying because there had been no rain for years. They looked like a few old sticks. It wasn't going to grab anybody's attention. Then I drew a storm with black thunderclouds and rain and zigzag lightning and some houses disappearing under a tsunami. It was better than the other drawings but it was still rubbish.

When the cricket ended, I decided to watch *The Simpsons*. I hadn't really enjoyed trying to design the poster. I hadn't come up with any brilliant images. It hadn't been half as much fun as making the card for Yasmin. I felt a bit sad that Yasmin was going to be away in London all weekend. It would be a bit lonely without her. Normally she comes round to my house, or I go round to hers, at least once on Saturday or Sunday. I wondered if we would ever be friends again. It all depended on whether I managed to find a set of walking teeth just like Gnasher.

Next day was bright and sunny and I tried to feel positive. Mum drove us into town and we parked the car and set off through the mall. Mothercare only had toys for little kids, cuddlies and educational bricks and stuff.

WHSmith had paints and pens and books but nothing like clockwork walking teeth. We went to Woolworths. There was loads of stuff there, but no Gnashers.

'You might just have to buy Yasmin something else,' Mum said in a rather tired voice, after we'd been walking in and out of shops for ages. I was getting hungry and I asked her if we could have lunch out in a cafe.

'Yes, why not?' said Mum when I suggested it. 'I'm absolutely shattered. Let's go to that little vegetarian cafe behind the cinema. We can have jacket potatoes. That's cheap and cheerful.'

As we were heading down the street towards the cinema, a new little shop caught my eye. *JOKE SHOP*, said the sign. My heart jumped with excitement. This could be it! I tugged at Mum's arm.

'Look!' I yelled. 'There's a joke shop! That's bound to have the teeth!'

'Your guardian angel must be working overtime,' said Mum. We went inside.

It was so cool. Instantly I vowed always to bring my pocket money straight here. There were the usual mock specs with dangly eyes. There was itching powder and whoopee cushions. There was a pig key ring, and when you squeezed it, poo came out of its bottom.

'Look at this, Mum!' I giggled, squeezing hard.

'Ugh, disgusting!' said Mum. 'We're not getting anything to do with toilets, Ruby. That would be tacky.'

'Pigs don't go to the toilet,' I said. 'Look at this flying piglet, then! You hang it from the ceiling!'

'Yasmin might like that,' suggested Mum in a hurry. I knew she was thinking about her jacket potato. She wanted to get out of there as soon as possible, but I wanted to spend loads more time in the shop. There were amazing costumes hanging up, wonderful joke hats and wigs. There were silver angel wings and a halo.

Mum went up to the counter. 'We're looking for wind-up walking teeth,' she said. The guy running the shop was thin and miserable-looking, which was the opposite of what you'd expect.

'Walking teeth?' he asked, frowning as if it was a stupid idea. 'No, sorry. We've got the chattering teeth, but they don't actually walk. We've got the walking hand of doom, though.'

He produced a green zombie hand, placed it on the floor and clapped his hands loudly. Instantly the hand started walking towards us. I screamed and ran away. It was amazing! Mum pulled a slightly disapproving face.

'Never fails,' he said. 'Women love it.'

'Well, this one doesn't,' said Mum firmly. 'This is a present for a little girl. I don't think it's quite suitable.'

The man picked up the hand and put it away. I was really disappointed.

'Oh, please can we have it, Mum?' I begged. 'Yasmin would *so* love it!'

'No,' said Mum firmly. 'What would her parents think of us if we gave her something ghastly like that?' She turned back to the shop assistant. 'Haven't you got anything suitable for little girls?' she asked.

'Well, there is this,' he said. He showed us an egg with a zigzag crack in it. 'You wind it up by twist-ing it, like this.' He demonstrated the winding,

then he placed the egg on the counter. It started to vibrate, then it split open and a little penguin came out and started to walk towards us. It was amazing and terribly cute.

'Right, we'll have that,' said Mum, getting out her purse. I was relieved that we'd found something that Yasmin would like and Mum was prepared to buy. But I was more worried than ever about what would happen when I saw Yasmin again on Monday and had to confess that I'd broken Gnasher.

Up till now I'd been hoping we'd find a set of teeth exactly the same, but now I had to admit we'd given up trying. Unless we organised a quick trip to the markets of Hong Kong, of course. As Hong Kong is literally on the other side of the world, I didn't think we could fit it in before Monday morning.

We also bought some special gift wrap with fish and octopuses on. It was sort of the same theme as the penguin, because penguins swim too. I started worrying about the penguins. We learned all about them last term in geography when we were doing Antarctica. I hoped all the ice in Antarctica doesn't melt, or the penguins would lose their home too.

Mum put the present and the wrapping paper safely away in her 'bag for life', which is made of hairy kind of twine, and we left the shop.

'Right!' she said. 'I'm absolutely starving, so let's see if they've got a table at the Lettuce Leaf.'

Thank goodness the cafe wasn't far away: just around the corner. We were walking so fast, we were almost running, and we bumped slap-bang into somebody just as we rounded the bend.

Omigawd! It was Yasmin! And her mum! They were supposed to be in London! I was so astonished, I couldn't say a word.

CHAPTER 13
I feel terrible

'HELLO! SAID MUM. 'We thought you were in London!'

Mrs Saffet looked puzzled.

'London?' she said, and glanced down at Yasmin, who went bright red.

'I thought we were going to take Granny to London like we did last time she was here,' said Yasmin, looking very uncomfortable.

'Oh – well.' Her mum still looked a bit mystified, but she seemed to want to move swiftly on and not focus on the muddle. 'Never mind. We've been a bit busy with my mother over from Turkey, but we put her on the plane home yesterday, so everything's settling down again.'

'Ruby really enjoyed Yasmin's party, didn't you, love?' said my mum. She's so polite. It was now my turn to blush. The mere mention of Yasmin's party had probably reminded everybody of the fabulous clockwork walking teeth.

'It was amazing,' I mumbled.

'Tell you what, Ruby,' said Mrs Saffet with her usual beaming smile, 'would you like to come over for tea tomorrow? Just a quiet couple of hours. I'm sure Yasmin would like to spend some time with you. It was all so hectic at that party.'

'I'm sure Ruby would love to come, wouldn't you, sweetheart?' said Mum.

I nodded. What else could I do?

'Say thank you to Mrs Saffet for her kind invitation.' Mum nagged.

'Thank you,' I murmured.

'They're both a bit shy today,' laughed Mrs Saffet. 'Before we know where we are, they'll be teenagers.'

'Oh, spare us that.' said my mum. 'It's bad enough having one in the house.'

Mrs Saffet agreed – because of course she's got

Yasmin's older sister Zerrin – and they went on about how it was murder living with teenagers, what with the moods and the door-slamming and stuff. Yasmin and I just looked at each other in a strange way. Yasmin didn't look as angry as she had last week at school, but she didn't look very friendly either. Maybe she was starting to turn into a teenager already. I began to dread tea tomorrow.

Except that I did have a fabulous clockwork penguin for her as a peace offering. I hoped it would be enough to console her for the loss of Gnasher.

Next day I wrapped the clockwork penguin's egg in the fish-and-octopus paper. I also made a small card showing a monkey looking sad, hiding under a leaf and with a tear running down his cheek. On the front I wrote *SORRY*, and on the inside I wrote *PLEASE FORGIVE ME, YAS-MIN, LOVE RUBY*. I didn't say what she would need to forgive me for. I knew I'd have to tell her face to face. In fact, I'd have to do it right at the start of my visit.

Mum drove me there. I held on tight to the card and present. It was like a re-run of last week-end, except that then I'd felt excited and couldn't

wait to get to Yasmin's. This time I had the sick sinking guilty feeling and wished the journey would take for ever.

'Don't worry, petal,' said Mum as she dropped me off. 'Yasmin will be fine about it, and she'll love the penguin's egg.' She gave me a kiss.

I felt a tiny bit better, but as I walked up Yasmin's path the sick feeling came back.

I rang the bell – the door opened. It was Zerrin. She looked more beautiful than ever. She was wearing some grey silk trousers and a black top, and earrings made of silver and pearl.

'Hi, Ruby!' she grinned. 'Come in! Yasmin's in the kitchen and she's got her speech all ready!'

What did she mean? I didn't like the sound of the speech, but Zerrin put her arm round me for a moment and gave me a little hug, so I felt at least she was on my side. Maybe Yasmin had prepared a speech saying she knew I had broken her teeth but it didn't matter, and she wanted to be friends with me again.

'Ruby's here!' yelled Zerrin.

I went through into the kitchen. There was a lovely smell of freshly baked chocolate cake. Mrs Saffet was making some smoothies with her blender, so there was a terrific noise. Then she switched it off, wiped her hands and said hello.

Yasmin was sitting at the kitchen table, looking pale. Her mum glanced at her and raised an eyebrow. It seemed like a kind of signal. Yasmin got up and came round the kitchen table. She looked at me and did a sigh and a sniff.

'Ruby,' she began. Her voice sounded small and shivery. Yasmin's voice is usually big and happy. This was a bit odd. Maybe she was going to apologise for our row last week. Yes, that would be it. 'I'm sorry, but I've got a confession to make.'

What? A confession? Surely I was the one who had a confession to make? Yasmin paused, sighed again, looked at her mum and went on.

'I'm really, really sorry, and I'm so sad about it,'
she said, 'but after the party last week Granny was
clearing up, and she took all the wrapping paper
out into the garden and burnt it. And we think
your card you made me must have been kind of
all jumbled up with the old wrapping paper
because we can't find it anywhere.'

I felt a sudden shock. Yasmin had lost my card!
I did feel a little stab of sadness at the thought of
it getting burnt, because I'd worked so hard on it
and it had meant so much to me. Huge tears gathered in Yasmin's eyes.

'I feel terrible,' she went on, 'because it was so
lovely, and I was going to frame it and hang it on

my bedroom wall, and it's the best thing anybody's ever given me, because you made it yourself and it meant so much and now it's gone!' The tears ran down her cheeks.

'Come on, Yasmin,' said her mum, offering her a tissue and putting her arm round her. 'No need for any more tears! I'm sure Ruby will forgive you.'

'Yes,' I said. 'Don't cry, Yas.' I gave her a hug. I still had to make my confession, but I thought I ought to give her the hug first — in case she didn't want to hug me after she'd heard what I'd done.

'I've got a confession too,' I said, once we'd finished the hug. Yasmin looked puzzled. I pressed on. I had to blurt it out now and get it over with. Poor Yasmin was feeling so guilty about my card. She needed to know I was feeling guilty too. 'Those lovely teeth you lent me,' I said.

Yasmin frowned — not in an angry way, but as if she couldn't imagine what was coming.

'I dropped them and fell on them,' I said. 'And they broke. Joe couldn't mend them, and we went around all the shops trying to find a set exactly the same, and we couldn't. I'm really, really sorry, Yas — please forgive me. I know they were your favourite present.'

'They weren't my favourite present!' Yasmin

burst out. She was still crying a bit. 'Your card was my favourite present! I haven't even thought about those stupid teeth all week! I've been too upset about losing your card!'

'So it doesn't matter at all about the teeth, Ruby!' said Mrs Saffet. 'Accidents do happen!'

'Anyway,' I said, 'I've got you something else to make up for it.' And I handed over the new present and card.

Yasmin was ecstatic when she saw the penguin come out of the egg and start walking towards her. And she liked the card so much, she gave me an extra huge hug.

'The penguin is so cute!' she yelled. It was nice to hear her yell again. It doesn't sound right when Yasmin is kind of whispering and guilty. 'I've forgotten all about the stupid old teeth!'

'And I've forgotten all about the card!' I said. 'And anyway, I can make another one any time you like!'

'Why don't you make something together?' suggested Zerrin, who had been watching from the doorway.

'Great idea!' said Mrs Saffet. 'After tea, instead of watching TV, we'll get a big bit of paper and you can design a picture together.'

'I know!' I shouted. 'The Poster Competition! The Save the Earth thing! We've got to hand it in tomorrow and if we win, they'll print it and it'll be stuck up everywhere to change the way people think!'

'Brilliant idea!' sad Yasmin, jumping up and down. 'We could have polar bears on it! With their ice melting!'

'And monkeys with their trees being cut down!' I added.

'It already sounds like a great poster,' said Yasmin's mum. 'But maybe you'd like some cheese salad first? And chocolate cake afterwards – just a teeny tiny slice?'

My tummy gave a huge rumble. At last I'd got rid of that sicky guilt feeling and now I was absolutely starving. It was weird that I'd thought Yasmin was angry with me all week, and really she'd been feeling guilty too.

'We must keep talking in future,' I said, 'so we both know what's going on and we don't have rows any more.'

'Ruby,' grinned Yasmin, 'you don't know what you're asking! Rows are my favourite thing in all the world – after you!'

'She'll have to be a lawyer when she grows up,'

said Zerrin as we all sat down. 'Then she can argue for money.'

'And what are you going to be, Ruby?' asked Mrs Saffet, offering me the cheese.

I shrugged my shoulders. I really haven't worked that one out yet.

'I'm afraid,' I said, 'I'm going to be greedy!' And I helped myself to a delicious little heap of grated cheese. Wow! This was the life.

Don't miss Ruby in her next
brilliant misadventure:

Ruby Rogers
Who Are You
Looking At?

Available now